Afghan Kid

Grumpy Grandpa

Text copyright © 2023 by Mokhtar Amin

Illustrations copyright © by Hunter Christian

All rights reserved. Printed in the United States of America.

For more information contact afghankid.org

ISBN: 979-8-9890894-0-6

The artist collaged watercolor paintings, hand sketched illustrations

and photographed antiqued textiles to create the imagery for this book.

Our town is called the dusty city because of the dust tornados. The land is dry, and the mountains are rocky. Nothing is green in our city except a few small trees.

Our tiny homes in the mountains are built from clay and rocks. The winds and dust often form dusty tornados and move from one neighborhood to another.

My fear of the dusty giants dissapears...

...as the tornados pass our home.

But I still fear two other things...

Grandpa and our Toilet.

We call him Grumpy Grandpa.
He is always grumbling and mumbling.

I am frightened to walk to the bathroom at night because it is far from the main house.

I haven't told anyone except my mother that I am afraid of the bathroom.

She tells me not to be scared of anything and to be a strong boy.

...So I use the lantern to brighten the path.

I always get nervous inside the bathroom because the toilet is a giant pit in the middle of the floor. I am scared that I could slip into the pit.

I nervously wait by the door because I am scared. But once I feel ready, I walk toward the toilet hole.

With my shaky legs, I lift one foot and place it on the other side of the hole. When I squat down, I avoid looking at the piles of gross pooh at the bottom. A stack of clay bricks and a hammer are next to me; Grandpa uses the hammer to break the bricks into smaller pieces. We have no toilet paper, so we use the brick pieces for wiping.

My Grandpa is in charge of

making the clay bricks for the bathroom.

Everyone in the family stays away from

Grandpa and his mumblings on brick-making days.

But I follow him because he needs my help,

and I want to learn how to make the bricks.

Grandpa always has all of the materials and tools ready before we start.

A pile of soil

An old shovel

Two water buckets

The heavy brickmaker

When the mud is ready, my Grandpa asks for the brickmaker, and I run to get it. I love learning how to make bricks. My Grandpa sees bricks, but they look like perfect little clay cakes on the ground to me. We leave the bricks on the ground so the hot sun can dry them.

When Grandpa is super tired, he lays on the Afghan carpet and asks me to **walk** on his back. My feet feel weird climbing on his back because we are supposed to respect our Elders.

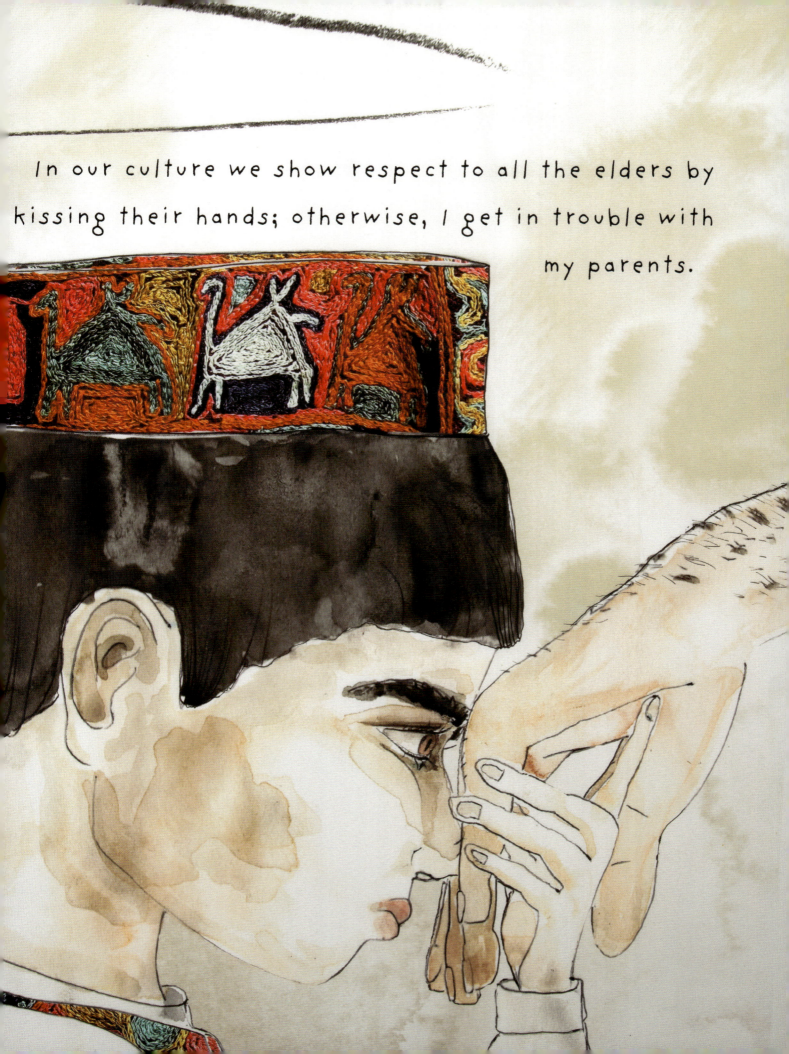
In our culture we show respect to all the elders by kissing their hands; otherwise, I get in trouble with my parents.

Even though I am afraid of the bathroom, my favorite time is in the afternoon. The sun shines through the small window, and I see tiny things floating in the dusty air. They look like little sea horses, tiny lizards, and flower pedals.

My
tiny
floating
friends make me less
afraid of the bathroom.

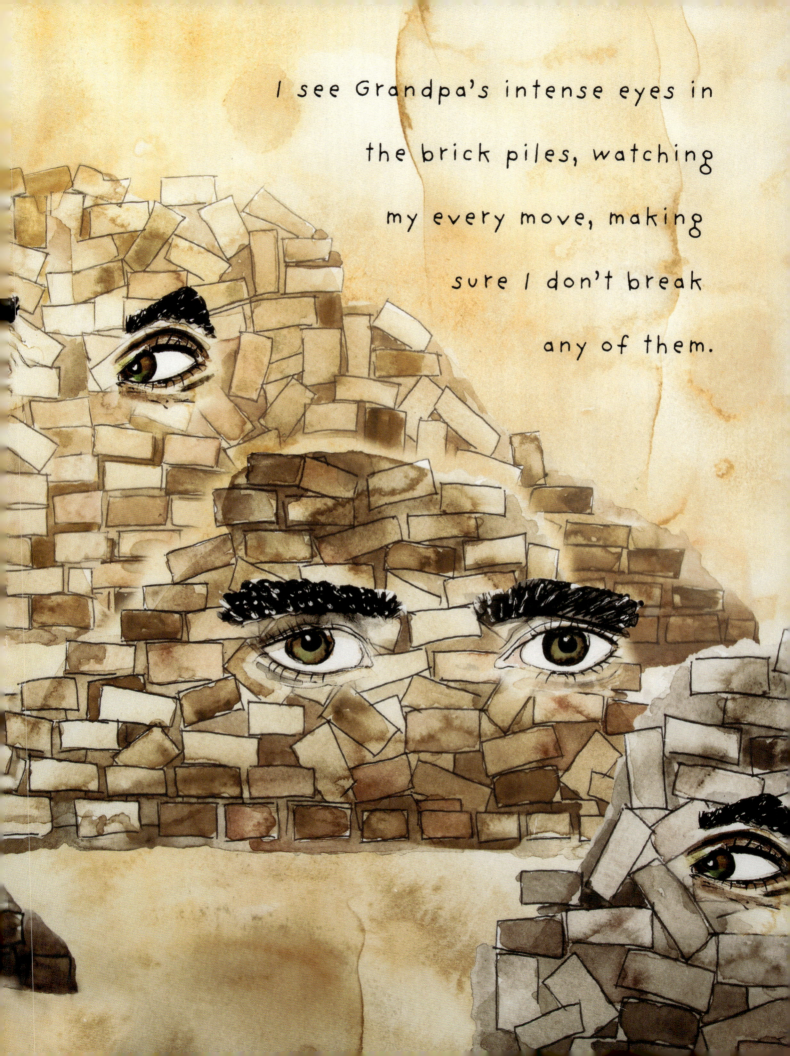

Every few months, a man and a cute donkey come to our neighborhood to clean out all the bathrooms. The man always has his sleeves rolled up and his pants stuffed inside his socks.

The donkey has two giant rubber bags on each side of his body for collecting the pooh.

I watch the pooh-cleaning from afar, but the gross smell is in the air, and the stinkiness goes up my nose. The donkey stayes in one spot, and the pooh pile gets higher with each shovelful.

Making the bricks and stacking them inside the bathroom makes me less scared of the toilet hole.

So my mother is right...

I am a **strong** Afghan boy.

Also,
the more time
I spend with my Grandpa,
I realize he is just a *little* grumpy but
always **loves** me.

The Afghan Kid book series is a collection
of my childhood experiences growing up in Afghanistan.

I dedicate these books and stories to the
children of Afghanistan.